Disney's
Winnie the Pooh
Use Your Words

If you're feeling blue or hurt

By something someone said,

Don't keep it bottled up inside.

Just use your words instead!

One breezy morning, Roo gobbled down his breakfast and raced out the front door as fast as he could. He could hardly wait to start the day.

He and Piglet were going over to Pooh's for a day of fun.

He was waiting outside for Piglet when Kanga
called to him. "Roo, it's a little cold out. Please come
back inside and get your scarf."

Roo pouted. "Oh, Mama! Do I have to?"

But Kanga insisted, so Roo huffed into his room.

"If you have something to tell me or want to share how you're feeling, please use your words, Roo," she reminded him.

"I'm mad because I had to come back inside!" Roo said.

"All right. But you still need to wear your scarf," Kanga said softly.

She lovingly wrapped the scarf around him just as Piglet arrived.
"Bye, Mama," said Roo, feeling much better.
And with that, he and Piglet headed for Pooh's house.

When Piglet and Roo arrived, Pooh was busy pulling his house apart looking for a missing honey pot.

Piglet offered to help Pooh. Soon the two friends got so busy that they forgot Roo was there at all!

"Hey, why don't we play a game?" suggested Roo.
"Perhaps in a little while," replied Pooh. "We're very busy."
"Well, can I help?" Roo volunteered.
But Pooh and Piglet were so busy, they didn't even hear Roo.

Roo felt very sad. His feelings were hurt.
He headed out Pooh's front door and bumped into Tigger.
"Hoo-hoo-hoo! What's new, little Roo?" Tigger called.
But Roo didn't give him so much as a nod.

"Why so glum, Chum?" Tigger asked, trying again. "Can't help ya if I don't know what's wrong. But whatever it is, I bet a good bounce would make you feel better!"

Not even bouncing could cheer Roo up.

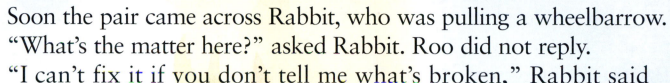

Soon the pair came across Rabbit, who was pulling a wheelbarrow.
"What's the matter here?" asked Rabbit. Roo did not reply.
"I can't fix it if you don't tell me what's broken," Rabbit said
kindly as he offered Roo an apple.

They each ate a crunchy apple, but Roo didn't feel any better. "How 'bout a little riddle?" asked Tigger. "What has stripes and bounces? Give up? Hoo-hoo-hoo! It's a zebra on a pogo stick!" But Roo didn't even smile.

"Why don't you fly your kite?" suggested Rabbit. "That should make your spirits soar!"

"Pooh and Piglet were gonna play with me today," Roo sniffled. The more he thought about it, the sadder he got.

Soon Eeyore strolled by and offered to help.
"You could use my tail for your kite," he said softly.
"Thanks, Eeyore," replied Roo. "But not even the
highest-flying kite in the world could make me feel happy today."

Rabbit and Tigger took Roo over to Owl's house.
"Ol' Beak Lips will fix you up," Tigger assured Roo.

"Well, I say now," remarked Owl, seeing Roo's long face, "you're a sad little fellow today. How about a story to cheer you up?"

But even though Owl's story was quite amusing, it didn't make Roo smile even a little bit.

When Roo got home, Kanga noticed that he was not himself.
"What's wrong, Roo dear?" she asked gently. "Are you still
upset from this morning?"

"No, Mama," he replied. "It's something else . . . It's Pooh and
Piglet. They were ignoring me!"
Then he told her what had happened at Pooh's house.

"If you were to use your words, what would you say to Pooh and Piglet?" asked Kanga.

Roo thought about it. "I guess I'd tell them my feelings were hurt," he said in a small voice.

"Then maybe that's what you should do," Kanga said, giving Roo a little nudge. "Go tell Pooh and Piglet how you feel."

So he hurried over to Pooh's house and said, "I have something to tell you."

Then little Roo took a big breath and cleared his throat. "I'm feeling really sad because you didn't pay attention to me today," said Roo. "And we never even had a chance to play together!"

"Oh, bother!" sighed Pooh.

"Oh, my!" gasped Piglet. "We never meant to hurt your feelings, Roo. Pooh, we were so busy looking for the missing honey pot that we forgot our manners."

"We are so sorry, Roo," said Pooh.
"We won't ever ignore you again!" cried Piglet. "We promise!"
Then Pooh and Piglet gave their little friend a great big hug.

Roo was so happy he bounced all the way home. Kanga and all Roo's friends were gathered around.

"Guess what! I did it!" he said, bouncing up and down excitedly. "I used my words to say just how I felt. And it worked!"

"Being honest about your feelings always works," said Kanga.
"I think you've learned a very important lesson today."

Suddenly Roo smiled from ear to ear. Expressing his feelings made him feel better than all the apples, stories and bouncing in the whole wide world.

"You know how I feel now?" Roo asked all his friends.
"We can guess," said Kanga, smiling. "But why don't you tell us."
"I feel really, really happy!" Roo shouted. "And from now
on I'm always going to use my words."

A LESSON A DAY
POOH'S WAY

Even little voices

should be heard.

Always say how you feel!